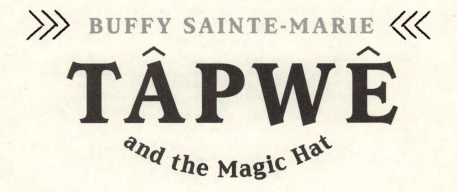

BUFFY SAINTE-MARIE

TÂPWÊ

and the Magic Hat

To the Piapot and Obey families
of Piapot Reserve and Regina, Saskatchewan.

Greystone Kids / Greystone Books Ltd.
greystonebooks.com

Cataloguing data available from Library and Archives Canada
ISBN 978-1-77164-546-1 (cloth)
ISBN 978-1-77164-547-8 (epub)

Editor: Linda Pruessen
Editorial consultant: Cherie Dimaline
Cree language consultant: Solomon Ratt
Copy editor: Dawn Loewen
Proofreader: Rhonda Kronyk
Jacket and interior design: Sara Gillingham Studio
Jacket illustration: Michelle Alynn Clement

Also available in Cree from Greystone Kids
tâpwê êkwa mamâhtâwastotin, translated by Solomon Ratt
ISBN 978-1-77840-024-7 (cloth) • 978-1-77840-025-4 (epub)

Printed and bound in Canada on FSC® certified paper at Friesens.
The FSC® label means that materials used for the product have been responsibly sourced.

Greystone Books gratefully acknowledges the Musqueam, Squamish,
and Tsleil-Waututh peoples on whose land our Vancouver head office is located.

Greystone Books thanks the Canada Council for the Arts, the British Columbia
Arts Council, the Province of British Columbia through the Book Publishing Tax Credit,
and the Government of Canada for supporting our publishing activities.

BUFFY SAINTE-MARIE

TÂPWÊ

and the Magic Hat

Illustrations by

Buffy Sainte-Marie &
Michelle Alynn Clement

GREYSTONE KIDS

GREYSTONE BOOKS • VANCOUVER/BERKELEY/LONDON

Contents

CHAPTER 1

A Gift

KAYÂS—ONCE UPON A TIME—there was a boy who lived in a town not too far from here. During the summer, the boy's mother was a student at the tribal college and did sewing to make ends meet. He stayed with his grandmother, who lived way out on the far edge of the reserve. He called her Kohkom, and she called him Tâpwê.

Tâpwê loved staying with Kohkom. He would wake up early to her soft morning song and smell the sweetgrass she burned as she thanked the Creator for the day. Tâpwê would help her with chores around the house. He'd pick up kindling for their wood stove, and dig and weed in the little garden where she grew potatoes and lettuce and squashes. Sometimes they'd even go fishing, and she would tell stories about long ago.

But Tâpwê was a little bit lonely. He missed his mom, and there were no other kids around out here to play with. That was kind of a nice change at first—Tâpwê didn't mind doing things by himself—but by the middle of the summer he was sort of wishing for a playmate or, even better, a dog to keep him company. They could have some adventures!

One day when Tâpwê was lying under a tree, watching the clouds, Kohkom called to him as she came down the steps from the little house. She held a big bowl of chokecherries and had a letter in her hand.

"âstam," she said. "Come here, my boy. Next week I go check up on your mother at the college. I want to help her out with her sewing while she's studying for exams."

Tâpwê smiled as he came to help Kohkom with her things. He knew his mother would be glad to have Kohkom around.

"I have some news you might like, Tâpwê," she continued as she set the bowl and the letter on the little table she used to pound chokecherries. "You're always wanting to go out adventuring across the valley. Well, your mom had a letter from our relative, Mrs. Ironchild, and she and her family would like you to come and visit for a while during their powwow. She hasn't seen you since you were a very little boy. And she has a bunch of kids—they're your second cousins. If you want, you can visit with them for a few weeks instead of staying in town with me."

Tâpwê's eyes opened wide and his face lit up. This was just what he'd been wishing for: an adventure!

"Oh boy!" he exclaimed. "Maybe they have a dog."

"Maybe," said Kohkom. "But there's a lot to do yet. If we get everything ready today, we can go first thing in the morning. It's a long drive."

Tâpwê and his kohkom set to work. Tâpwê began to gather firewood as Kohkom sat down in front of her special flat boulder and spread out the chokecherries they'd picked the day before. Using a smooth stone, she pounded and pounded the cherries until they were as smooth as peanut butter. Then she added a little sugar and some fat and pounded some more. Finally, she divided the mixture into small portions and wrapped each one up in cloth, like a little package. Tâpwê watched her as he worked. He could hardly wait to have a taste.

After he'd stacked up a huge load of firewood, Tâpwê went over and sat down on the ground next to Kohkom. She opened up one of the packages of cherries and they each had some.

"Mmm," Tâpwê said. He nodded toward the pile of wood he'd stacked up alongside the house. "That's for when you get back."

"Oh my!" she answered, seeing how much he'd stacked. "That's real good, boy. Thank you. Oh, but I'm sure gonna miss you while you're gone visiting. You're my favorite grandchild."

The night before they were to leave, Tâpwê was wide awake with excitement. He was used to camping outside next to Kohkom's house, but not with new people way across the valley. Would he like the Ironchilds? Would his second cousins be nice? Would they have adventures together? He thought he wouldn't be able to sleep, but then, before he knew it, he was smelling sweetgrass and hearing Kohkom singing her morning prayer song. Tâpwê knew this day was the start of his adventure, so he jumped out of bed, eager to get washed and dressed.

In the kitchen, Kohkom was gathering the last items for their trip. Tâpwê helped her carry bags to the old truck.

"I've packed up some cherries for Mrs. Ironchild, and a few other things," she said, handing him one last bag as he climbed into the front seat and buckled up.

Kohkom got in next to him. Then she reached into the back seat and retrieved a big bundle of cloth. She gave it to Tâpwê.

"I have two gifts for you," she said. "Open the first one."

Tâpwê gently unwrapped the bundle. Inside was something he'd never seen before. At first he had no idea what it was. Then he saw that it was a strange-looking hat, like the feather headdresses the old chiefs wear, but smaller and kind of upside down. It was made out of feathers and woven porcupine quills. On the top were three little bluebirds and three baby grass snakes, who were pink and purple. At first Tâpwê thought they were toys; but then, believe it or not, they fluttered their little eyelashes and stretched. Tâpwê gasped.

"Kohkom! An chaa!" he said, rubbing his eyes in disbelief.

"It belonged to me when I was your age," Kohkom said. "Go ahead and put it on."

Tâpwê put on the hat. It felt funny and made him laugh, and when he did, the little creatures began twittering and bouncing up and down. That Magic Hat wiggled and whistled and chirped and sang!

"But Kohkom," said Tâpwê, "they're not tied down! Won't they get away?"

Kohkom looked at the boy in the Magic Hat and laughed.

"They're there of their own free will, my boy," she said.

"My mother saved the birds from an icy frost one spring. And those poor little grass snakes were out in the hot summer sun and couldn't find any shelter, so she tamed them. They're grateful to us. They can help you find your way and keep you company on your adventure. Be good to them and they won't have any reason to leave you."

》》————《《

The ride to the Ironchilds' reserve was long, but Tâpwê didn't mind. He had so many questions about the Magic Hat, and Kohkom was a good storyteller. She told Tâpwê about some of the adventures she'd had with the Magic Hat when she was a little girl.

"The first time I understood that the Magic Hat was truly alive was the first day I wore it—just like you— but I was out picking berries, not riding in a car." She laughed. "At first, I thought the animals were toys. I'd been walking along for a little while, getting used to the feeling of having this strange hat on my head, when I heard a noise. It sounded like someone was yawning— *ho-hum*."

Tâpwê laughed as Kohkom stretched and yawned as if she'd just woken up.

"I looked to the right; I looked to the left; I looked ahead of me; I turned around and looked behind me," Kohkom said, "but I didn't see anybody! I was so puzzled. So I sat right down and began to unfasten the Magic Hat."

Tâpwê took the hat off his head and stroked it gently as Kohkom continued her story.

"If I hadn't already been sitting, I might have fallen right down when one of the birds spoke to me," she said. "And do you know what he asked me?"

Tâpwê shook his head.

"He asked me if we were there yet!" Kohkom laughed and laughed—and Tâpwê knew why. That was his favorite question whenever they went on a long drive.

"My mama hadn't mentioned a word about talking animals," Kohkom continued, "so you can imagine how surprised I was! And then one of the snakes spoke too! She yawned and told me that they'd all been sleeping. That was Prrr." Kohkom pointed at the Magic Hat in Tâpwê's lap. "She's the littlest snake—pink as a sunrise and with long eyelashes.

"That's when one of the other bluebirds, whose name was Piyêsîs, told me that she'd been dreaming. 'I dreamed about him again,' she said, with a faraway look in her eyes.

And all of the others agreed. They'd dreamed of 'him' too!"

"Who was 'him'?" Tâpwê asked.

"Good question," said Kohkom. "I had no idea who they were talking about! I just held the Magic Hat in my lap and listened to the racket the creatures were making!"

Kohkom's eyes were on the road in front of them, but she snuck a look at Tâpwê as she imitated the noises the birds and grass snakes had made: "*Chirp-tweet-sssss-whistle-buzz-ch-ch-ch!*"

Tâpwê laughed as he imagined the hat singing, with all the creatures flapping and bouncing around.

"And then, all of a sudden," Kohkom continued, "Piyêsîs put her wings up in the air and asked the others to be quiet. They all stopped talking and listened.

"Tss, the purple grass snake, told me to put the Magic Hat back on. So I did. And I listened too.

"Not a sound. But then I heard something moving around in the bushes up ahead.

"'I hope it's not a bear!' I whispered.

"Piyêsîs heard me. 'I hope it is!' she replied—and the others agreed!

"*Oh no!* I thought. *Please. . . not a BEAR!* I hadn't planned for *that* kind of adventure!"

CHAPTER 2

The Sîwinikan Bear

KOHKOM STOPPED HER STORY. Just when it was getting exciting, Tâpwê thought.

"Then what happened?" he asked, hoping she would keep going.

But she just smiled at him. "I'll tell you some more later," she said as she pulled the truck off the highway at a rest stop. Together they found a parking spot near an old chokecherry tree with a picnic table underneath. Kohkom reached into the back seat for the bag of snacks she'd packed, and they sat under the green leaves and blue sky, eating carrots and apples and drinking juice. Then, after a little stretch, they returned to the truck. Once they were on their way again, Kohkom got back to her story about her adventures with the Magic Hat.

"Well, there I was picking berries, worried that a bear was going to come crashing through the bushes, when all of a sudden I heard something very strange," she told Tâpwê.

"*Deedley deedley deedley deedley!*" Kohkom's voice went all high and light as she tried to imitate the sound.

"Someone was singing!" she said. "I didn't know who it could be. The birds from the Magic Hat began to flap their wings again, making the headdress jump and wiggle.

"I took a deep breath," Kohkom continued. "*Who is that?* I asked myself. But the only answer I got was the song—*deedley deedley deedley deedley.*"

"Who was it?" asked Tâpwê, but Kohkom didn't answer right away. She just kept telling her story.

"Piyêsîs, the middle-sized bluebird, was the first one to answer. 'It can't be him,' she chirped. The youngest snakelet, Ch-ch-ch, let out an excited little hiss. 'Maybe it *is*,' she whispered. Then the Magic Hat began to flap and flutter almost off my head as everyone started shouting about berries, and how much 'he' loved them!

"'Who loves berries?' I whispered as loudly as I dared. I was still worried about bears, but I couldn't stand it for one more single minute that everybody but me knew what was going on—especially since I was in charge of the transportation!

"This time, it was the oldest bluebird, Okimâw, who answered me. 'It must be the Sîwinikan Bear,' he sang. 'Don't be scared!'"

Kohkom's eyes twinkled as she glanced over at Tâpwê, eyebrows raised. "I had no idea what the bluebird was talking about. I knew about black bears and brown bears and grizzly bears, but I'd never heard of a Sîwinikan Bear. The bluebird explained. 'The Sîwinikan Bear,' he said, 'the Sugar Bear! He's called by many names but hardly ever seen.'

"Shy little Ch-ch-ch told me that the Sîwinikan Bear is the sweetest little bear in the forest, and that her mommy had told her about the bear when she was no bigger than a potato blossom. The littlest bluebird, whose name was Tweep, said she'd always thought the bear was pretend, even though she wished he was real! And all at once, the creatures began to sing."

Kohkom's sweet old voice filled the truck with the song she'd learned so many years ago.

He's Sîwinikan Bear with his little black eyes
He's Sîwinikan Bear with his little black eyes
And he brings all the children a sweet surprise
He's Sîwinikan Bear   Way heyo hey-yo!

He's Sîwinikan Bear with his teddy bear ears
He's Sîwinikan Bear with his teddy bear ears
And he calls all the children "my darlings, my dears"
He's Sîwinikan Bear   Way heyo hey-yo!

He's Sîwinikan Bear with his yummy-num lunch
He's Sîwinikan Bear with his yummy-num lunch
He's got picnic and berries and saskatoon punch
He's Sîwinikan Bear   Way heyo hey-yo!

He's Sîwinikan Bear with his Deedley song
He's Sîwinikan Bear with his Deedley song
He goes "deedley deedley deedley deedley" all day long
He's Sîwinikan Bear   Way heyo hey-yo!

"Wow!" Tâpwê said when Kohkom finished singing.
Kohkom continued. "Oh my, wow indeed, and now I
could see why those animals were so excited. Because
all around us were little footprints and other signs that
somebody had been gathering berries and cherries and
saskatoons. And, sure enough, somebody was up ahead

singing *deedley deedley deedley deedley*, which, when you think about it, is rather a unique song.

"We looked up the path. The little footprints went leading on, clear as day—and there, right at the spot where the footprints ended, was a wiggly patch of berry bushes. I tiptoed down the path. UP popped the Sugar Bear! He was fluffy and brown, about the size of a great big puppy and just as cute.

"'Tânisi!' I said, my mouth hanging open.

"'Tânisi, my dears!' said the Sîwinikan Bear, stepping out of the bushes pigeon-toed with a basket of berries over his arm, very happy indeed to see me and the Magic Hat.

"'Ohhhh!' I said, because—you're not gonna believe it—but I was sure that the little bear had been brown before. And now he was white.

"'I've been waiting for you,' said the Sîwinikan Bear. 'My darlings, I thought you'd never catch up. My, but you're slow!'

"I told the little bear that I'd been afraid he might be fierce, and that I had almost run away. This made him giggle, and when he did, he turned a sunny shade of yellow, and then to the color of a peach, right before my eyes!

"'An chaaaa!' said that little bear. 'See how you are?

Look—the picnic is all ready. mîcisotân! Let's eat!'"

Kohkom described how the Sîwinikan Bear reached into his picnic basket and began to spread out the contents on the ground. That basket was pale green and smelled like sunshine.

Tâpwê looked at his grandmother, his eyes wide. "Sweetgrass!" he whispered.

"That's right," said Kohkom. "And out from that sweetgrass basket came branches and branches loaded with berries—more branches than any ordinary basket could ever hold. There was even a pitcher of saskatoon punch, big enough for all of us to share. The Sîwinikan Bear turned from cloud pink to baby blue and back again. 'My darlings,' he said, 'this is for us all.'

"As I looked at the food the Sîwinikan Bear was sharing with us, I thought about the chokecherries my mama and I had pounded that morning. There wasn't very much, but I reached into my pocket and laid the little package in front of the Sugar Bear.

"'Mmmm-megwetch! Thank you,' exclaimed the little bear. 'My favorite thing—generosity!' And he smiled a rainbow smile that filled the field with colors. I thought I would turn inside out with delight! We even forgot

about being hungry. We turned around and around watching the colors change, and wherever we looked we saw the Sîwinikan Bear. We played slide-down-the-rainbow twenty-four times before we finally decided to eat our lunch—and was it ever good. Then we all decided to take a rest in the shade."

CHAPTER 3

Two Sweethearts

"BY THIS TIME, the Sîwinikan Bear was as green as grass. We were all cuddled together in the shade of a berry bush, looking up at the clouds that floated through the sky, when the Sugar Bear pointed at one.

"'There's the Trickster,' he said.

"'Where?' we asked.

"'That cloud up there, see?'

"He pointed his finger at a cloud, and we watched as it turned yellow. First it was the shape of a coyote. Then it looked more like a raven. Then it looked just like a great big rabbit. The Sîwinikan Bear began to sing.

My darlings, my dears:
Some call the Trickster Coyote;
Some say the Trickster's a bird;
Some call the Trickster a rabbit;
Some say the Trickster's absurd;
My darlings, my dears, how he changes
From people to people he's new;

Wâpos on the loose is the Trickster
Trickster Haa Yaa Yaa!

"When the Sîwinikan Bear had finished singing,
Piyêsîs fluttered her wings and asked if he'd ever met
the Trickster. '*Hoo-wee!* Many times,' replied the little
bear, who was brown and fluffy again. 'I knew him quite
well long, looong ago. His shoulders weren't all skinny
like that rabbity cloud up there. Oh no. Back then he
had big wide shoulders, like a man.' The Sîwinikan Bear
looked around, and then he whispered: 'He also had two
sweethearts!'"

In the passenger seat, Tâpwê began to giggle. It was
hard picturing someone who looked like a rabbity cloud
having even one sweetheart, never mind two. Kohkom
explained that having two sweethearts wasn't the worst
problem—at least according to the Sîwinikan Bear. The
problem was that the Trickster didn't love either one,
and that was bad. He just liked to make them get jealous
of one another.

"That Trickster would sneak up on those two
girlfriends and listen to them say how handsome he was
and argue about which one of them was his favorite,"

Kohkom explained. "One time, the Sugar Bear told us, all the people were sitting around the fire, just enjoying life. The Trickster was sitting in between his two sweethearts. He had charmed and flirted with each of them so much that they were both just cra-zy with love.

"When the Sîwinikan Bear told us that," Kohkom said, "he rolled back his eyes and patted his heart." She gave her own heart a thump-thump pat, just like a heartbeat.

"That Trickster felt one girl edge in closer to him, and then the other one, again and again and again, which was just what he wanted; but he pretended not to notice and just kept on making eyes at an old lady across the fire, who ignored him. Pretty soon he was just skwunched in between those two girlfriends. And, you see, he liked that!

"But just then: *ker-RACK*!"—Tâpwê jumped a little in his seat as Kohkom imitated the sound—"there came a flash of lightning. The Trickster tumbled backward off the log and ran and hid in the bushes, not caring a bit for anybody but himself. Finally, the girls caught on that the Trickster had been treating the two of them like fools all along. They both deserted him and went back to being friends, and later they married each other's brothers and lived happily ever after. And all the Trickster has to show for his foolishness are his narrow, skinny shoulders."

Kohkom scrunched up her shoulders toward her ears and laughed. "Anyway, that's what happened the day I first wore the Magic Hat and went out to pick berries," she said. "I met the Sîwinikan Bear. And I learned a thing or two about the Trickster."

Tâpwê and the bluebirds and the grass snakes all smiled at Kohkom as she drove.

"Tâpwê, I said I had two gifts for you," Kohkom continued. "One is the Magic Hat. The other is some advice: watch out for Tricksters!"

Tâpwê nodded, but he wasn't really paying attention. He was much more interested in the Magic Hat than in advice. Also, he felt about ready for a nap. They'd been driving for more than four hours, and the rocking of the old truck was making him sleepy. Outside the window, the countryside had changed from very flat to pretty little hills. Tâpwê closed his eyes for a few moments, until he felt the truck slow down and turn onto a bumpy old dirt road.

"There she is," said Kohkom, pointing to a spot up

ahead where a lady waited by a big rock. "That's Mrs. Bull. She's the auntie of your mom's cousin Mrs. Lilian Ironchild, who invited you to visit."

When Kohkom stopped the car, Mrs. Bull came over and gave her a hug through the driver's-side window. Then she reached over to shake hands with Tâpwê. In his lap, the Magic Hat was very quiet. The creatures looked like sleeping toys.

"Oh, you're gonna have some fun here, Tâpwê," said Mrs. Bull. "I want to sit here and visit with your kohkom a little before she goes. My niece Lilian is expecting you. She's got a house full of kids—just down that trail and up beyond the top of the hill. The kids are all getting ready for the powwow. But after a while I have to go feed my son Sam's mama dog. How about you play along the trail here for a while until I come and get you. Then I'll walk you there. It's on the way to Sam's house."

A dog! Tâpwê looked at Kohkom, who smiled and nodded.

"Okay," Tâpwê said to Mrs. Bull. "megwetch, Kohkom," he said as she leaned over to hug him goodbye. Then he got out of the truck and started down the trail.

CHAPTER 4

Parsnips and Potatoes

TÂPWÊ WALKED ALONG THE TRAIL. He was carrying the Magic Hat and all his other stuff. He put everything down beside a tree. He yawned.

He looked at his magic headdress. It didn't look very special right now, just sort of limp and lumpy, like a pile of old clothes in a corner. All the little animals were snoozing.

"*Tweep*," snored one of the bluebirds. The baby grass snakes didn't even buzz. They just lay there. . . like three noodles.

"*Chirp*," said one of the bluebirds.

"Oh *chirp* yourself," teased Tâpwê. "I thought birds woke up early, but here it is afternoon and you're sleeping."

Now they all began to wake up from their naps. The bluebirds stretched their wings and yawned. The grass snakes started their exercises, changing shape from an O to a C to a Q to an S.

Pretty soon everybody was wide awake and ready to restart the day. The bluebirds hung on while Tâpwê put the Magic Hat on his head. The snakelets decided to ride in Tâpwê's shirt pockets, and they made up a game.

"Close your eyes, Tâpwê," said Tss from his place in Tâpwê's left pocket, "and go in the direction we wiggle."

"We're gonna steer you," said the other two snakes, from the pocket on the right. "Don't worry—we won't let you fall in any gopher holes!"

Tâpwê closed his eyes. *Tssss*, he heard, and in his left-side pocket he could feel the snake bouncing. So Tâpwê turned left, and just missed a clump of red prairie flowers. Then he heard *ch-ch-ch-ch-ch* from his right-side pocket, and felt the snakes wiggling, so he turned right. This got them all heading north again, walking alongside a tiny stream that crossed the path.

Tâpwê thought they must be almost to Mrs. Ironchild's house by now, but he couldn't really tell. Those little grass snakes wouldn't let him peek; they had a surprise for him, they said. Finally, after some whispering in his pockets, the snakes told him to stop. "Okay, Tâpwê," they said, "now look down and dig!"

Right at his feet was a big patch of green leaves.

"Potatoes!" he said. "And parsnips too! I'll dig some up and bring them to our relatives!"

And he did. And as he dug, the birds sang a cooing song, and here's how it went:

> *Friends there are, up ahead*
> *Friends there are, up ahead*
> *We will arrive in safety,*
> *bringing gifts to those who welcome us,*
>> *Haa Yaa.*

CHAPTER 5

A Powwow Welcome

NOT FAR AWAY, three little girls were standing at the edge of the path, looking for porcupine quills to sew on their dresses. One looked up and saw the boy in the beautiful Magic Hat.

"An chaaaa!" she said in wonder.

"Auntie, come quick!" yelled another, and very soon Tâpwê found himself surrounded by wide-eyed people, smiling at their visitor.

"We knew someone was coming," said the woman who had come when the girls called. "That must have been you we saw down there raiding last year's garden."

"Your garden?" said Tâpwê, handing her his big armload of parsnips and potatoes. "Oh no, I'm sorry! I thought these were wild! I meant them as a gift. . ."

Tâpwê let his words trail off. He felt silly, bringing somebody a present from their very own garden!

"megwetch," said the woman. "Thanks for gathering these. Every bit helps. We're starting a powwow tonight, and we hope we'll have a lot of visitors."

She smiled at Tâpwê. "And who are you?"

"My name is Tâpwê. My kohkom is visiting with Mrs. Bull. I'm on the way to find Mrs. Ironchild—she's my mom's cousin. I guess I took the wrong path."

"tânisi, Tâpwê!" The voice came from behind Tâpwê, and it belonged to a tall woman with a big smile. "I'm Mrs. Ironchild, but you can call me Auntie Lilian. And you're in just the right place. You must have taken the shortcut." She put her arm around Tâpwê's shoulder. "Come, we're expecting you. I haven't seen you since you were a little wee boy. My, but you've grown."

Tâpwê felt a little shy. He didn't really remember his relatives, so he just acted very polite. The little creatures on his hat were quiet and perfectly still. Maybe they were feeling shy too.

Just then Mrs. Bull came down the trail and joined them. "Well, I see you got here," she said to Tâpwê. "Sylvia's boy!" she said to Auntie Lilian. "My goodness, he's big now, eh?"

Auntie Lilian agreed.

As Tâpwê walked into the village with Auntie Lilian and Mrs. Bull, he could see that everybody was busy getting ready for the powwow. At each house they passed, people were gathering berries, preparing food, cleaning and cooking, getting out their dance outfits, and stretching the hides on the big drums.

When they finally arrived at the Ironchilds' house, the door opened and out came a whole group of children, all dressed up and ready for the powwow. One by one, Auntie Lilian introduced them.

"Tâpwê, this is Winston, and Thelma, and Rose, and Thomas," she said, pointing to each in turn. "Oh, where's that Willie?"

Just then, a boy about Tâpwê's size came out from behind the house, all loaded down with folding chairs and willow backrests.

"Oh good, there you are," said Auntie Lilian, waving to the boy as she headed off toward the house. "Willie, come here and meet Tâpwê—and then the two of you take those chairs over to the powwow grounds. I'm real busy."

"tânisi!" said Willie Ironchild, real friendly. "You got here just at the right time, Tâpwê. You can help me carry chairs!"

For the first time since he'd left his kohkom's truck, Tâpwê smiled his big, friendly smile. And when he did, the birds and the little grass snakes on his hat fluttered and wiggled and chirped and whistled and sang. This commotion surprised Willie Ironchild so much that he sat down fast—*WUMP!*—right on his bottom.

Tâpwê helped Willie up and then helped him pick up chairs. Willie was taller than Tâpwê but he looked to be about the same age. And he had a bandage on his toe. Tâpwê was just about to introduce Willie to his Magic Hat friends when a loud *BOOM* sounded from down the path.

"Come on!" said Willie. "They're getting ready for the Grand Entry!"

"*Boom boom boom boom BOOM!*" The big drum sounded again over at the powwow grounds.

Willie and Tâpwê had their arms full of chairs, but they hurried as fast as they could go. Willie couldn't take his eyes off that hat. This made Tâpwê laugh, and then the Magic Hat laughed too. Two girls in fancy dresses all decorated with sparkling beads passed them and exclaimed at Tâpwê's hat. Willie was too busy staring at the Magic Hat to notice the girls' beadwork, but Tâpwê did. It was beautiful!

At the powwow grounds, a large arbor of cut trees had been set up to offer shelter from any weather that might come along. At the far end, lots of dancers were already lining up.

"Here, Mrs. Cheechuck," Willie said as he handed a woman two chairs. "Oh, and this here's Tâpwê."

"megwetch, Willie. tânisi, Tâpwê!" said Mrs. Cheechuck, exclaiming "Chaa!" as she noticed the Magic Hat. When Tâpwê said "Pleased to meet you" and smiled his friendly smile, it seemed like she wanted to say more, but somehow she couldn't. She just looked and looked at Tâpwê and his hat, with her mouth open and no words coming out. The boys laughed as they hurried off to deliver more chairs.

There were really a lot of people. Singers were all gathered around their big drums, and women were unwrapping their shawls as the music started.

Boom, boom, boom, boom, boom went the drum, just as nice and steady as can be, and ten singers sang strong and loud: "*Haaa Yaa, Ay Ha haaa yaaa.*" Down at the far end of the arbor, the dancers started to file into the arena, one after the other.

Everyone in the crowd stood up except for the drummers, and Tâpwê and Willie put their chairs aside as the first person entered the arena.

He was an old man. He wore a beautiful big feather headdress that trailed down over his back, and he proudly carried a long, curved staff out in front of him. Tâpwê noticed that eagle feathers were tied all down its length.

"That's Mr. Kaiswatum," whispered Willie. "He's an Elder. He knows everything about the old ways and medicine and stuff. He told me that Eagle Feather staff is like our Cree flag."

Tâpwê nodded, though he'd never heard that before. He watched the way Mr. Kaiswatum came into the arena, leading all the others in a line behind him. He danced slowly in time to the drum—not fancy, just real humble himself—while he held that Eagle Feather staff up proudly for all to see.

The little animals on Tâpwê's hat were excited, but they stood at attention, quiet and all eyes as the old man led the dancers around the arena.

First came the oldest. They danced to the slow, steady rhythm of the drum as if they were praying. To Tâpwê, that drum felt like his own heartbeat, strong and powerful and alive.

Fathers came in next, and then mothers, with shawls wrapped around their shoulders. The long fringes almost reached the ground, and their beaded moccasins danced

to the heartbeat sound. Then came the young men, followed by the young women. They danced like their Elders. My, they looked good!

"Traditional dancers," said Willie. "But just wait!"

Into the arena came a group of girls whose dresses were decorated with rows of jingling rolled tops from tin snuff cans. "Jingle Dancers," Willie said.

Now they heard a new sound! Bells were jangling, and into the arena came red and blue and yellow and purple. In came green and orange and bright, feathery pink!

"Fancy dancers!" said Willie. "That's me someday! I was gonna dance this time, but I whacked my toe on a rock last week."

And were those fancy dancers ever fancy! They had feathers tied into their hair. They had beaded arm bands and belts, and they had great big brilliant feather bustles on their hips and shoulders. Some wore shaggy sheepskin leggings, and they all wore bells around their ankles: some cowbells, others sleigh bells, or tin cones. What a sound they made as they danced!

Now, Kohkom had told Tâpwê about powwows, but hearing about it wasn't the same as being there. This was loud! This was bright, and this was fun! The girls were dancing in beadwork of every color in the rainbow. Even the littlest children danced around and around the arena, led by old Mr. Kaiswatum.

Then the music stopped, and so did the dancers—*BOOM!*—right on the beat.

Everything was suddenly quiet. Mr. Kaiswatum said a long prayer. Some of the dancers found chairs and sat down, but then the music started up again, this time fast and exciting. Now even the animals on the Magic Hat bobbed up and down to the beat.

The people danced and visited late into the night, telling jokes and having fun with old friends and relatives, eating berry soup and bannock and corn on the cob and other good things. The little animals on Tâpwê's hat were very polite, but there were so many people who wanted to see them that after a while they cuddled down and took a nap under the feathers of the Magic Hat. Willie and Tâpwê watched the powwow for a long time. Then they went out and clowned around outside the arena with Winston and Thomas, Willie's older brothers. Finally, they joined right in, dancing a couple of easy rounds. They didn't have any fancy clothes or feathers, but they did have Tâpwê's Magic Hat,

which—once the little creatures woke up—caused a
sensation. Bouncing back from their nap, now those
little animals danced right along with the excitement
of the powwow. Tâpwê felt happier than he ever had
in his life to find these new friends, and his smile was
grateful and sincere. Those boys sure had a good time
that night, and so did everybody else. Tâpwê met all of
Willie's friends and relatives, and he didn't feel shy at
all anymore.

Then the Eagles looked down from the sky overhead,
recognizing the old songs their ancestors had taught the
people long, long ago.

And as the music rose and fell to the heartbeat of the
drum, the Eagles high in the sky sang in harmony with
the song of the human beings, giving thanks for all the
good things of the world.

CHAPTER 6

Wâpos the Trickster

SOME DAYS WERE BUSY with things to do, and some were lazy.

On the busy days, Tâpwê helped his new friends haul water from the river, and chop wood, and things like that. Willie Ironchild was the most fun, Tâpwê thought. Willie had a little dog named Brownie who loved to come along and keep the boys company whenever they worked or played together.

On the lazy days, the Magic Hat's bluebirds and grass snakes sometimes curled up with Brownie under a tree when it was time for a nap. Tâpwê just loved that dog.

But today Willie was busy with his own chores, so Tâpwê—wearing his Magic Hat—was out gathering wood by himself down by the stream. It was an awfully hot day. He was taking a break, leaning his back against a shady tree, when he heard a voice.

"tânisi, Tâpwê!"

The voice belonged to Wâpos, who was standing near the stream, not too far away.

"tânisi," said Tâpwê, giving the creature a good look. He hadn't met Wâpos before, but he knew he was sometimes called Rabbit. And now he could see why. He looked sort of like a person but also a bit like a rabbit—though not any rabbit Tâpwê had ever seen. And he was tall, like a grown-up, but different. For one thing, he was furry. For another, he seemed playful—like a kid. He sure was strange.

"It's hot!" said Wâpos, in a dill-pickley voice. "Let's go down to the river and cool off, pick some lily roots for supper."

"O-kay," said Tâpwê. He was curious about Wâpos, and he was thinking how good it would feel to swim in the cool river where the lily roots grew.

And so off they went, Tâpwê in his Magic Hat, and Wâpos. Tâpwê didn't notice that the Magic Hat was *very* quiet.

Not too far away, the Ironchilds' neighbor Mr. Cheechuck and his brother-in-law, Mr. Rockthunder, were fixing Mr. Cheechuck's roof. They saw Tâpwê and Wâpos going off together and slowly shook their heads.

"That Wâpos," said Mr. Cheechuck.

"Uh-huh!" said Mr. Rockthunder. "I hope young Tâpwê is ready for the Trickster."

Pretty soon Tâpwê and Wâpos were at the river.

"I know!" said Wâpos. "Let's race in and see who can pick the most lily roots for supper! You better take off that fancy hat and put it on the riverbank. Don't wanna get it wet."

The animals on Tâpwê's hat didn't like the sound of

that, and the grass snakes began to protest. But Tâpwê was too hot to pay attention.

"Let's go!" he said. He set his hat by a tree and jumped into the cool river.

But do you know what happened?

That Wâpos just grabbed the Magic Hat and plunked it on his own head, then took off in the other direction.

"Now the Magic Hat is mine!" Wâpos cheered as he ran. "Now every time I smile, the birds will sing and the grass snakes will dance, and I, Wâpos, will be even more important than ever around here!"

Balancing the Magic Hat on his head, and grinning his sneakiest grin, Wâpos went striding into the village, with Tâpwê trying to catch up.

"Ho! Wâpos!" shouted Mr. Cheechuck from up on his roof. "You foolish thing! Everybody knows that's not your hat. You must have tricked Tâpwê. And that's no way to treat a guest!"

Wâpos grinned a lopsided grin in an attempt to wake up the hat, the same way it woke up when Tâpwê smiled. He tried all kinds of smiles. But the Magic Hat didn't sing, or wiggle, or whistle, or anything. It just sort of lay there on top of Wâpos's head, limp as old socks. Wâpos took off the hat and put it down on the ground.

"Chaa!" said Wâpos to the men on the roof. "You are absolutely right." And then he pretended to cry. "Boo hoo hoo hoo! I am so ashamed. What a thief I am! I should just throw myself to the dogs. . . let 'em chew on me for a while. Maybe that'll teach this old Trickster a lesson!"

And that's just what he did. Mr. Rockthunder's dogs were all barking and jumping and carrying on like crazy. Wâpos did a somersault and four big handsprings—and went sailing right into the middle of all that noise!

But in a flash those noisy dogs were fast asleep and snoring, and Wâpos went skipping off down the path again singing, "TRICK-ster, Ha-Yaa-Yaaa!"

Wâpos knew a whole lot about magic himself, you see.

The people watching just shrugged their shoulders and shook their heads. They were used to Wâpos by now.

But poor Tâpwê didn't understand at all, and when he got back to Willie's house—his eyes still all red from crying— he was m-a-d. Willie's big brother Winston, who had seen everything, told Willie about how Wâpos had charmed the dogs.

"Don't mind Wâpos too much, Tâpwê," Winston told him. "That's just how he is."

But even though he had his Magic Hat back again, Tâpwê did mind. Very much!

CHAPTER 7

Thelma's Frybread

SUPPER AT THE IRONCHILD HOUSE sure was different from supper with Kohkom, Tâpwê found out. There were so many people! There were Auntie Lilian and Uncle Alvin Ironchild, and Winston and Thomas, and Rose and Thelma, and Willie and Tâpwê and Mrs. Loudhawk, the children's grandmother. There were lots of bowls on the table, and big pots of food, and a whole lot of talking going on. Even the animals on Tâpwê's Magic Hat, which was hanging on a hook on the wall, were chattering away. It was noisy!

Uncle Alvin spoke up, loud enough to be heard over the others. "I was talking to Sam Rockthunder today. That nice dog of his is gonna have puppies soon."

Tâpwê's ears woke to attention.

"Oh boy!" exclaimed Willie. "I hope he saves a good one for me!"

"Just what we need around here," teased Thelma. "Another Piggy!"

"My dog's name is Brownie, not Piggy!" said Willie.

"Anyway," continued Uncle Alvin, "Sam also told me you had a run-in with Wâpos, Tâpwê."

"I sure did," said Tâpwê, "and I'm real mad at that guy!"

The other people at the table chuckled, which Tâpwê didn't think was very nice at all.

"Hey, remember what Wâpos did to Thelma last winter?" said Winston. "That was the winter Thelma learned to pay attention, *ayyyy*." He took a big bite of frybread and made a funny face, and all the children laughed.

Tâpwê was eager to hear all about Thelma's experience, but Auntie Lilian had a rule: no Wâpos stories until the supper dishes were all done. Tâpwê would have to wait, at least for a bit. And so they ate their supper and chatted about some other relatives who were coming to visit the next week, and then they all pitched in to clear the table.

Later on, as Willie's brother Thomas was folding up the dish towels, he finally got to telling the story. "That ol' Wâpos," he said, "he sure got Thelma that time, didn't he, Thel?"

Thelma Ironchild looked down and laughed.

"tâp-wê!" she said as she laughed with her sister, Rose. Tâpwê smiled. He knew they weren't laughing at him. For

as long as he could remember, he'd known that "tâpwê," besides being his name, also meant "Yes, indeed," "right on," "true," and "for sure." It was kind of fun having a name that did two jobs.

"Hey, Tâpwê," said Rose. "I hope you ain't been bragging."

Tâpwê hadn't been bragging, and said so to Rose. But he didn't know what that had to do with Wâpos.

"See," Rose explained, "what happened is, one time all of us girls were making this quilt together? A buncha boys came over, and Thelma got to bragging about how good she could make frybread. So that Rodney Sesap—he was the one Thelma liked then—he says, 'Why don't you just go ahead and fix some up for us.'

"So, of course, Thelma's thinking here's her big chance to show off. She gets the fire going and mixes up the batter, and drops them doughs into the hot oil. And it's all smelling so good that we're all just hungry for some of Thelma's braggart frybread, *ayyy*!

"And that's when Wâpos comes in—just as Thelma's putting her frybreads in the basket to cool. So Wâpos gets Thelma to talking about something, and soon enough, he has her believing that somebody's outside looking for her. So she goes looking out the door and forgets all about her basket of frybread, see?"

Tâpwê *could* see; in fact, this story was starting to sound awfully familiar.

"Of course, there was nobody there. Wâpos was just distracting her, eh?

"Now," Rose continued, "we don't know how Wâpos swapped baskets on her, but he did. All I know is when Thelma takes the towel off her basket of frybread, we're all looking at a basket of old dried-up horsebuns instead! Thelma never has bragged on nothing after that!"

They were all laughing now, Thelma most of all.

"So, don't ever brag, Tâpwê," Rose said. "But actually, after it was all over, I had to admit. . . Thelma's real frybread was gooood!"

"Oh my, yes," said Mrs. Loudhawk, who'd been listening and laughing along with the rest of them. "Thelma's a good cook. You know, Tâpwê, I had some trouble with Wâpos one time too."

"What did he do to you?" Tâpwê asked. He was still mad at Wâpos for stealing the Magic Hat, even if he couldn't help but laugh about Wâpos's trick on Thelma.

"Oh, it was a long time ago," Mrs. Loudhawk said.

"I had spent the whole afternoon pounding chokecherries on a little table outside. I went in the house for a rest before supper, and when I came back to my table, my pounding stones were just as I left them, but my cherries were gone.

"I hollered at Winston—he was only small then—and asked him if he'd gotten into my chokecherries. Winston said he hadn't.

"Still, they were gone, and I was mad. 'Who could have taken them?' I wondered. Children? Crows? They couldn't just disappear! 'Aha!' I finally said to myself. 'Wâpos! It's just like Wâpos to eat up all somebody's chokecherries, even though he knows how long it takes to pound them nice like I do!'"

Mrs. Loudhawk told the children that she'd found Wâpos and asked him, and that the Trickster promised he hadn't eaten even one cherry all day. And when she saw that his mouth wasn't cherry-stained, she believed him.

But that wasn't the end of it.

"My husband was changing his shoes to go in the house," Mrs. Loudhawk continued, "when all of a sudden he jumped up in the air with his foot stuck straight out. And then he started yelling at me, which he didn't usually do.

"'Mrs. Loudhawk, my dear!' he yelled. 'What have you put in my moccasin?'

"And there, sure enough, were my chokecherries, all stuck to my dear husband's toes."

In the Ironchilds' kitchen, Winston danced around on one foot and wiggled his toes!

"Wâpos hadn't eaten any chokecherries, it's true, but he was the cause of the mischief all right, as usual." Mrs. Loudhawk chuckled. "And sure enough, we could hear old Wâpos laughing at us, out in the trees."

But Tâpwê wasn't laughing.

"I just don't understand why everybody puts up with that old Wâpos," he said when the merriment had simmered down. "It seems to me that he only causes trouble!"

Mrs. Loudhawk laughed kindly. "Wâpos is our very own Trickster, Tâpwê. By and by you'll understand. He keeps us alert, that Wâpos. I should have put my cherries away when I went in the house. I'm just lucky a bear didn't find them first and bust up the whole yard!"

Tâpwê and Willie lay awake that night talking about Wâpos until finally Thelma Ironchild threw a moccasin at them. That only made them giggle.

"Go to sleep, you kids!" Auntie Lilian said. "You got to get up early tomorrow, Willie. It's your turn to do chores."

Tâpwê closed his eyes. He thought about what Mrs. Loudhawk had said. Maybe he had been too trusting of a stranger. He could have lost his Magic Hat forever if a real thief had been around, instead of just silly old Wâpos. It was a good lesson to learn—and one that might save him some trouble down the road. As he drifted off to sleep, he did so with a new fondness for the strange, rabbity Trickster.

CHAPTER 8

Upside Down

THE NEXT MORNING AFTER BREAKFAST, Tâpwê went outside to play in the dirt awhile. He was hoping that maybe Wâpos would come by. He thought he'd like to know more about the mischievous Trickster, now that he understood him better.

The birds and grass snakes sat around in a tree next to Tâpwê's dirt pile, taking it easy. The dog was sleeping.

"Do a trick for me!" Tâpwê said.

The little animals looked at each other blankly. The dog just kept on sleeping.

"We don't know any tricks, Tâpwê," said Piyêsîs.

"Oh," said Tâpwê, and he sighed, feeling bored. It seemed to him that Magic Hats ought to be able to do magic tricks. Maybe later he and Willie could train this little dog—Brownie or Piggy or whatever his name was—to do some tricks. Tâpwê, anyway, was in the mood for some adventure. He wondered what Wâpos was doing today.

"Did you guys know Wâpos before we came here?" Tâpwê asked the bluebird.

"Not exactly," said Piyêsîs from the branch above Tâpwê's head.

"But we'd heard stories about him," said Ch-ch-ch.

"Tell me!" Tâpwê begged, climbing up onto the branch.

"Do you know how Wâpos got those skinny, narrow shoulders of his?" asked Piyêsîs.

"No," said Tâpwê eagerly, even though Kohkom had already told him that story.

"Well," Piyêsîs continued, "in the old times, believe it or not, Wâpos had wide, handsome shoulders. He also had *two* sweethearts!"

"HO!" said a big voice just beneath them.

"*Wuff!*" barked the little dog in surprise. The birds were so startled that they all flew up into the air, and the little snakes came jumping into the pocket of Tâpwê's shirt.

"Wâpos!" Tâpwê shouted happily, forgetting all about Piyêsîs's story. "I was just wishing and hoping you'd come by. Let's go play!"

"Come on, then," said the Trickster. "I, Wâpos, know all kinds of great games! We shall play Possum and Bat." They all set off down the hill through the woods, in the direction of the coulee.

The grass snakes still loved to ride in Tâpwê's shirt and steer him to the best sticks whenever he'd go to gather firewood, so they were glad when Wâpos headed for the woods. The whole group played follow-the-leader until Wâpos finally stopped next to a medium-sized tree.

"Attention, attention!" Wâpos announced. "This is the official Possum and Bat tree! Tâpwê, you can be the possum and I, Wâpos, shall be the bat. Hurry now, hup-hup-hup! Up the tree! Out on the limb! Now we hang from our knees like a kite in the breeze, and we begin."

Tâpwê was hanging upside down by his knees pretty well, but the poor little snakes were having a terrible time trying to stay in his pocket.

Bomp! Bomp! Bomp! Out they fell. Tâpwê was so glad to be learning a new game with the famous Wâpos that he didn't even notice. But the bluebirds did.

"How do we play?" asked Tâpwê.

"Just tell why Possum is better than Bat, of course," said Wâpos.

"Oh. Of course," said Tâpwê, who didn't want to look stupid in front of his new friend. "Possum is better than Bat. . . because. . . uhh. . . because Possum has warm fur?"

"Sheee!" said Wâpos. "Bat is better than Possum because

he doesn't have any fur to get fleas in! Hoo hooo! I win!"

The bluebirds all tried playing Possum and Bat, but they were no good at hanging upside down. And the grass snakes didn't like this game at all. They were too little to wrap around the limb of Wâpos's official Possum and Bat tree, and whenever they'd fall off, Wâpos would laugh and point at them. Tâpwê laughed at them too. The little dog just looked bored and lay down to take another nap.

So, while Tâpwê played Possum and Bat upside down with Wâpos, the little animals waited patiently nearby until the game was over.

But then Wâpos wanted to have a stand-on-your-head contest. (He did push-ups with his ears!) And after that he wanted to do backward somersaults down the steepest hill on the reserve. Nobody could do as many somersaults, backward or forward, as Wâpos the Trickster.

None of this was any fun at all for the snakelets or the bluebirds, but do you know. . . Tâpwê didn't even care. He seemed to have forgotten all about his patient little friends who couldn't do any tricks. He just ignored them and kept right on playing with Wâpos, as if they were too little to be any fun for cool guys like them.

Day after day, Tâpwê and Wâpos played together. They stood on their heads and did hundreds of somersaults and hung upside down. Even though Tâpwê didn't like this upside-down business any more than his hat friends did, he looked up to Wâpos more and more. It was as if the Trickster was some kind of wonderful big brother.

If you want to know the truth, Tâpwê was just too shy to tell Wâpos that he couldn't take any more upside-downing. He just did whatever Wâpos wanted to do.

And, as the days went by, what Wâpos seemed to want was to be Tâpwê's only friend. It seemed to be working, too.

Willie Ironchild noticed the difference. Tâpwê paid no attention to what Willie wanted to do. Instead, he just waited around for Wâpos and played whatever Wâpos wanted to play.

Tâpwê even ignored his friends on the Magic Hat. He hardly ever included them in his play anymore, and he began to think of them as silly little-kid things. . . like baby toys that he'd outgrown.

Tâpwê just wanted to be like Wâpos.

CHAPTER 9

More About Wâpos

A FEW DAYS AFTER Tâpwê and Wâpos first played Possum and Bat, Wâpos was off on business of his own. Willie and Tâpwê each had a big bucket of river water in their hands. As soon as they'd delivered the buckets to Willie's mother, who was washing the floor that day, they could go and play.

"I know," said Willie when they were done. "We could go over and visit Mr. Kaiswatum. Remember him from the powwow? He's the one who said the prayer."

"Okay," said Tâpwê.

"Come on. Put on your Magic Hat and let's get going."

"Magic Hat? Ha!" said Tâpwê. "This stupid hat can't even do one trick. I don't know what's so 'magic' about it anyway. The Trickster is more fun any day. Hey, maybe Mr. Kaiswatum knows some Wâpos stories!"

"Tâpwê, Mr. Kaiswatum knows more stories about everything than anybody else around here—or anyplace else, I bet. But if he tells us any stories about Wâpos, you just better listen good! Wâpos is a real Trickster, you know."

"I know that," said Tâpwê, kind of cranky. But he put

on his Magic Hat and off they went, with Willie's dog tagging along.

Now, Mr. Kaiswatum always did like dogs. As a matter of fact, he had given Willie his dog in the first place when it was just a pup, and he called him Kâsakês. Kâsakês was at that special frisky age between being a puppy and a dog. He was fat, and mostly brown, with some black and white on him. The name *kâsakês*, Willie had told Tâpwê, meant "greedy guts," because this dog would eat all of his own dinner and then want everyone else's.

"Kâsakês!" Mr. Kaiswatum called when he saw them coming. "How is little Kâsakês? Do you still eat everything in sight?"

"He sure does," Willie said. "My sister calls him Piggy, but I just call him Brownie."

"So you have a dog with three names, do you? That's pretty good."

"I wonder where Wâpos is today?" Tâpwê said. He wasn't interested in talking about dogs right then.

Mr. Kaiswatum slowly shook his head.

"Oh, you never can tell about Wâpos," he said. "He comes and he goes. He's a very strange creature. He's very, very old, you know."

"He is?" said Tâpwê.

"Older than you?" asked Willie.

"Oh my, my, yes!" said Mr. Kaiswatum with a laugh. "Even my grandfather, long, long ago, knew Wâpos. The old man used to tell me all kinds of stories that he'd learned from *his* grandfather, who said that Wâpos is a very ancient Supernatural."

"You mean like the Great Spirit?" asked Tâpwê. "My kohkom told me that the Great Spirit is everywhere at once and has always been here. She said that even the Creator is part of the Great Spirit, and the Creator made everything! Even the Sky and the Earth. . ."

Willie joined in, stretching his arms out wide. "And the Sun and the Moon and the People and the Animals and everything!"

"I believe that's right, boys," said Mr. Kaiswatum. "But Wâpos isn't at all like the Great Spirit. He can't create anything. He can only mix things up that are already here."

The bluebirds and snakes on Tâpwê's hat were listening to Mr. Kaiswatum, too. Every once in a while Tâpwê would hear an *uh-huh* or a *chirp* or a *ch-ch-ch*. They were testifying, as if they knew that what the old man was saying was right.

"I don't know why the Creator gave Wâpos that power," said Willie.

"I don't know either," said Mr. Kaiswatum. "But Wâpos surely is powerful in his own way."

The little snakes had been whispering to the bluebirds while the old man and the two boys talked about Wâpos. Now, suddenly, the birds on Tâpwê's hat cried out.

"*C-caaww*," they yelled. "*C-caaww! C-caaww!*"

"*C-caaww! C-caaww!*" came an answer from the trees nearby, and down flew a big old black crow!

"What's going on?" asked Tâpwê.

"Oh, that's just Âhâsiw. He sounds funny now, but he's really quite a nice fellow. Poor Âhâsiw. Before they got mixed up with Wâpos, his ancestors used to be beautiful songbirds. But my, how he's changed. He knows that the thing about Wâpos is you have to pay attention when he's around. Sometimes he'll trick you and sometimes he won't."

Mr. Kaiswatum continued, "Boys, if you learn to keep alert around Wâpos, the rest of life becomes a lot easier. But if you don't—if instead you're like Âhâsiw here—your whole life can change just because you were a little careless."

Right at the moment, though, Tâpwê wasn't really listening. He was watching Brownie watching a bug. The dog was down on his front paws with his tail end up in the air like he wanted the bug to play, but the bug flew away.

"Wâpos is like a walking, talking accident-about-to-happen," Mr. Kaiswatum was saying, "and you never know when. I suppose these little birds want to hear about how Wâpos changed the crows?"

Now Tâpwê was listening again.

"But I don't want to bore you boys," Mr. Kaiswatum said with a twinkle in his eye. "You don't like stories, do you?"

"Sure we do!" said Willie and Tâpwê. "Please tell us a story."

"Well, all right," Mr. Kaiswatum said. "kayâs, kayâs—this was a very long time ago, you understand—Âhâsiw the Crow wasn't as we know him now. He was the best singer around these parts. Silver, he was, too. Just beautiful, shiny, glowing silver. And he was so kind and so pleasant to have around, everybody just loved him. The other animals always used to invite him to share in their dinner.

"One evening Wâpos was roasting some meat over the fire. Âhâsiw came by to pass the time and enjoy the good weather. He wasn't even hungry. Well, it happened that

74

Wâpos needed to go down to the stream for some water, so he asked the crow to fan the fire a little now and then so it wouldn't go out. Âhâsiw promised he would.

"For a while, Âhâsiw did a real good job of tending that fire. But Wâpos, that Trickster, was taking an awfully long time coming back. You see, down at the stream Wâpos had come upon some ladies, and as you probably know, that old Wâpos, he always likes to get some attention by charming the ladies!

"Well, now, pretty silver Âhâsiw flew up into a tree near the fire to keep an eye on it, but Wâpos was taking so long that, by and by, the crow fell asleep. When he woke up, he heard Wâpos coming through the woods. Âhâsiw the Crow, he just flew down out of that tree and started fanning that fire as fast as he could, because it was just about out. He got it going, all right, but fanning so close and so fast had covered his beautiful silver feathers with dirty black soot!

"Wâpos was mad! He was real hungry by now and he thought his dinner would be all cooked, but it wasn't! Wâpos called Âhâsiw a lazy old thing, and all sorts of other mean names. And then he turned Âhâsiw the Crow black—forever! Even his descendants would never be

silver again. And as for the crow's beautiful singing? It was no more. Ever since that time, the crows have been trying to cough that soot out of their lungs."

"*C-caaww!*" said the crow up in the tree nearby.

The little snakes and bluebirds wiggled and chirped in sympathy for poor Âhâsiw the Crow. But Tâpwê was thinking: "Wow, that Wâpos is powerful!"

"Poor Âhâsiw," said Willie.

"That's not the worst of it," said Mr. Kaiswatum. "After Wâpos had changed the crow, nobody recognized him at all! And when they heard that awful noise he makes now, the other animals didn't want him around anymore. They thought he would surely wake up their babies, and they were afraid of the different-looking stranger that their old friend had become. So now the crow has to make his living mostly by stealing scraps and leftovers."

Willie had some frybread in his pocket and he tossed it over to Âhâsiw. The crow ducked—he was used to people throwing rocks at him. But when he came closer and saw what it was, he ate up the frybread and then hopped on over to have a chat with the bluebirds. After that, Âhâsiw even tried riding around on Tâpwê's hat. Tâpwê took great big funny steps like Wâpos. You should

have heard Willie Ironchild laugh! Willie's laughter even
made Âhâsiw laugh, which was something he hadn't
done for a long time, and the Magic Hat was all merry.

"Well, you boys are very good visitors," Mr. Kaiswatum
said. "If you come inside, I'll give you both a little treat.
But you'd better leave that Kâsakês pup outside. There's
not enough for him too."

And that's when Tâpwê got his first taste of maple sugar.

Now, maple sugar was real hard to get in that part
of the country, and Mr. Kaiswatum sure did like it!
Whenever old friends from those reserves out east came
to visit, they knew just what to bring as a gift for the nice
old man: a big chunk of sweet, brown sparkly maple sugar.

And maple sugar is just what got Tâpwê into trouble a
few days later!

CHAPTER 10

Maple Sugar

IT WAS A VERY NICE AFTERNOON, and Tâpwê and Wâpos were taking it easy under a big tree, telling stories. This was the first time that Tâpwê had left the Magic Hat behind. He'd hung it on a hook at the back of the house and walked away, just like that.

Now, the trouble with Wâpos's stories was that Tâpwê never could tell if they were true, or just things Wâpos *wished* were true. One day, he'd asked Wâpos that very question.

"Do you believe what I say is true?" the Trickster had asked, looking hopeful.

When Tâpwê said he wasn't sure, Wâpos explained how his storytelling worked.

"If you *wish* my stories are true, that's good," he'd said. "And if you *believe* that they are true, it's even better. But the best of all is when you *act* as if they are true."

That, Wâpos said, was when stories actually became true. Wâpos told Tâpwê that his imagination was power, and that if he could just get enough people to act as if something were true, then it would be.

Tâpwê found this very confusing. He never could seem to tell the difference between Wâpos's "wishes" and downright lies. Today was no different.

"Of course, you know about the Sun Dogs," Wâpos was saying. Tâpwê had been watching Mrs. Sesap off in the distance, hanging out clothes on her clothesline.

"No," said Tâpwê. "What's that? A story?"

"It's no story at all!" said Wâpos. "Everybody around here knows about Sun Dogs. Just two winters ago, it was a real cold afternoon—*brrrr!*—and up in the sky, there they were: the regular sun in the middle of the sky, and then two other little suns, one on the left, and one on the right. Three suns in the sky at the same time. Honest! You can even ask Mrs. Sesap over there. She saw them at the same time I did!"

Tâpwê decided to test Wâpos. He got up and ran across the meadow to Mrs. Sesap's yard.

"Mrs. Sesap, did you and Wâpos really see three suns in the sky at the same time?"

"Why, yes, we did, Tâpwê. It was the Sun Dogs. It isn't very often that anybody gets to see that, but every now and then it does happen. The light has to be just right. My daughter Missy and my son Rodney saw them too."

Tâpwê thanked her and went back to Wâpos under the tree.

"See?" said Wâpos. "I told you. Sun Dogs."

Tâpwê couldn't help noticing that as he spoke, Wâpos was making all kinds of slurpy eating noises. Tâpwê looked at Wâpos. When he noticed what the Trickster was holding in his hand, Tâpwê's eyes popped open.

Wâpos stopped talking and grinned a great big rabbity grin. He narrowed his little red eyes and wiggled his ears in two directions and his eyebrows in two other directions, and said, very slowly, "Ma-ple su-gar!"

Tâpwê looked at the maple sugar and remembered that taste. He watched Wâpos with such longing that Wâpos finally broke off a tiny corner and gave it to him. "Old Man Kaiswatum has gone to town for a few days to visit his daughter. He said he has lots of maple sugar and that I should just help myself."

That one tiny bite of maple sugar is what did it. Tâpwê just had to have some more.

"Go get some for yourself!" Wâpos told him. "The old man has plenty; he won't even miss it. I'm going home now." And Wâpos hopped away, singing a very old song most everyone else had forgotten long ago.

Now, Mr. Kaiswatum's house just happened to be right on Tâpwê's way home, so he went over and sat on the porch steps for a while. He could just about taste that maple sugar.

Then Tâpwê went to the door and knocked, but there was no answer. It seemed Wâpos had been telling the truth about Mr. Kaiswatum being away.

Finally, Tâpwê couldn't resist, and he tiptoed in. There, on a shelf in the kitchen, all wrapped up just like before, was the package Mr. Kaiswatum had opened when he shared the treat with Tâpwê and Willie. Tâpwê looked over both shoulders. He felt like a thief, in spite of what Wâpos had told him.

He got the maple sugar down off the shelf, cut off a little piece, and put it in his pocket. Then he rewrapped the package and put it back. And then he got out of that house as fast as he could and ran off down the road.

>>———《

Things continued to go downhill after that. For one thing, Tâpwê went back for more maple sugar—three times! For another, he no longer seemed to have any interest in the animals on his Magic Hat. He would only stop and notice them now and then, as if they were old toys. Most of all, though, Tâpwê continued to try to be like Wâpos, and to compete with him, and to impress him. Even when Tâpwê played with Willie, he was always talking about Wâpos.

CHAPTER 11

Turned to Toys

AROUND ABOUT THIS TIME, the Ironchilds' relatives came to visit, and the big kids put up a small tipi in the backyard for all the children to sleep in. Tâpwê could see how glad Willie was to see his favorite cousin, Marvin.

"This is my new friend," Willie said, introducing them. "His name is Tâpwê, and he's our relative, and he comes from way across the valley, and. . . well, you're not going to believe this, but Tâpwê has this Magic Hat, and the hat has real birds and little, tame grass snakes on it."

"Come on," said Marvin. "You're joking me again, Willie. I know you."

"He'll show you!" said Willie. "Soon as we get these bedrolls into the tipi!"

But Tâpwê didn't help with the bedrolls or wait to show Marvin his Magic Hat. Instead, he headed down to the coulee with Wâpos. They started hanging upside down, playing Possum and Bat. Tâpwê finally had a turn at being Bat.

"Possum's better because Possum can hide in a hollow log!" Wâpos was teasing.

"No, Bat is much better, because Bat can fly around at night and catch mosquitos!" Tâpwê teased back, real sassy.

"Ho!" said Wâpos. "Who wants to fly around at night catching mosquitos, anyway? What a dumb thing to want to do!"

(Tâpwê wondered why, no matter whether he was Possum or Bat, he never could get the better of Wâpos.)

"Tâpwê, come on!" hollered Willie as he and Marvin came running down the hill. "Come show Marvin your Magic Hat!"

Tâpwê was glad not to have to play Possum and Bat with Wâpos anymore. To tell the truth, Tâpwê was beginning to think that Possum and Bat was kind of a stupid game. It always made him feel bad. Right now, he felt like he could use some attention himself, and he thought that his big smile and his Magic Hat were just the things to get him some! The three boys went back to the tipi, where all of Willie's relatives were admiring what a good job the children had done putting it up.

Tâpwê got his hat from off the hook at the back of

the house and put it on. Then he looked at his reflection in the window and practiced his smile. Boy, he just couldn't wait to see their faces!

"Hey, everybody!" Willie said. "This is my friend Tâpwê from the other side of the valley. Look at his Magic Hat!"

Tâpwê paused for a moment. Then he held his head up high and slowly walked into the middle of the group, smiling a great big smile and turning his head from side to side. Everybody was quiet and polite, like they were waiting for something special to happen.

And do you know what happened?

Nothing. Nothing at all.

There was an uncomfortable silence. Tâpwê could sense that something was wrong.

He tried to smile even bigger, and then he waited. . . and waited. But still nothing happened.

Finally Willie's aunt Marie spoke. "Oh, how cute," she said. "A pretty hat with toys on it."

The people all said Tâpwê's toy hat was very nice. And then they went back to admiring the tipi.

Tâpwê turned away. He felt so embarrassed. But then a feeling of terror began inside him. As calmly as he could, he walked back over to the house. He took off his Magic Hat and looked at it.

"Oh no!" he cried. His eyes filled with tears and he began to shake. "Ohhh no! It can't be true!"

But Aunt Marie was right. The bluebirds and grass snakes had turned to toys.

CHAPTER 12

A Medicine Song

TÂPWÊ LAID HIS HEAD against the wall of the house. He couldn't think straight. What was going on? His hands were cold and tingly, and he felt like he was in a nightmare and couldn't wake up. Suddenly, he bolted away down the road toward Mr. Kaiswatum's house—but he sure wasn't after maple sugar this time. He knew he could be alone there, and he needed some time to think.

A few minutes later, he sat down next to Mr. Kaiswatum's tiny woodpile. He held the Magic Hat in his hands and looked at it again. Then he touched Piyêsîs. She was as cold and as hard as a toy made out of wood. So were the others. Poor little Ch-ch-ch was frozen in the shape of an S.

What could he do?

"I'll never see them alive again," Tâpwê whispered. He shivered and gritted his teeth.

He remembered his kohkom's second gift—her word of advice: "Tâpwê, watch out for Tricksters!"

Of course! This was Wâpos's doing—like when he

turned the crow from a pretty silver songbird into a black-feathered old croaker.

Then Tâpwê had a terrifying thought.

"Oh no!" he said out loud. "Maybe *I'm* about to turn into a toy too! It would be just like Wâpos to. . . oh no!"

He began to cry, his shoulders shaking with his sobs.

Tâpwê laid his head down on the soft feathers of his Magic Hat and let the tears run down his face. In his head he could hear a song. He kept his eyes closed and listened. Someone was singing—strong and loud.

How strange! It sounded sort of like Eagles far off in the distance, though other singers were echoing the song—and *their* voices sounded like the birds and grass snakes on his hat! Tâpwê listened carefully to the words of their song:

You listened to that other
You listened to that other
Now you've forgotten how to dance
to your own heartbeat, Haa Yaa

Tâpwê lay very still.

My own heartbeat? he thought. He stopped crying. Could he be dreaming? He listened as hard as he could.

That way is right for the Trickster
That way is right for the Trickster
You'd better use what the Great Spirit
gave to you and you alone, Haa Yaa

Of course! All of a sudden everything made sense. Ever since he'd met Wâpos, Tâpwê had been trying to be just like him!

Then something else dawned on him. The friendship of the creatures on the Magic Hat had brought out the best in Tâpwê—that was what made it magic. But Tâpwê had turned mean on them when he decided to become friends with Wâpos.

If only I had been nice to them too, Tâpwê thought. *We could have all been friends if only I had tried. Now it's too late.*

But the song continued:

You'd better do what YOU want to do
You'd better be what YOU want to be
Be who YOU want to be
You are YOU, haa yaa. Haa Yaa!

CHAPTER 13

A Lesson

TÂPWÊ WAS SOARING WITH THE EAGLES. Below, he could see himself on the ground, and he could see Mr. Kaiswatum coming up the road, smiling and humming a tune.

"But what's this?" he heard Mr. Kaiswatum say with a smile. "Look at all this kindling wood on my woodpile! It must be that someone in the village has been gathering kindling wood all day."

Then Mr. Kaiswatum rushed over to the small, still body on the ground behind the woodpile. The animals on the Magic Hat didn't move.

"Tâpwê! Tâpwê!" he cried, patting Tâpwê's cheek. "Oh, what's happened here, boy?"

Tâpwê was deathly still. Mr. Kaiswatum shook the boy, but there was no response.

Then, suddenly, Tâpwê was back on the ground and taking a sharp, deep breath. He opened his eyes to Mr. Kaiswatum's relieved face looking down at him.

"Why, Tâpwê!" Mr. Kaiswatum said. "The sun's about to go down, boy! You're gonna catch a cold, sound asleep on the ground. You scared me to death! Are you all right?"

Tâpwê slowly sat up. His Magic Hat was all crooked on his head, and his eyes were red and puffy from crying.

"What's wrong, boy?" Mr. Kaiswatum said.

"Oh, Mr. Kaiswatum," said Tâpwê. "I feel funny. . . like I've been in another world." He took a deep breath before he continued. "I have something to tell you. While you were away, I went in your house and took some of your maple sugar. Wâpos told me it was okay to do it, but I can't blame Wâpos, because in my heart I knew it was wrong. But I went ahead and took it anyway, and then I even stole some more—three other times.

"Oh, I've been feeling very sick in my heart these days! I didn't notice it until just now, but I guess I've been changing into someone like Wâpos. Even the animals on my hat have changed. I treated them like they were just toys instead of real friends, and now they've really become toys!" He held up the hat for Mr. Kaiswatum to see. "I can't believe I threw away their friendship. Their friendship is what made the Magic Hat magic! I know that now, but it's too late."

A tear slid down his cheek.

"Anyway, I stacked up all this firewood for you, to try to pay you back for stealing your maple sugar. And then

I had this dream, and I heard this strange, strange song. I was so scared at first, but then, after the Eagles sang to me, I wasn't scared at all anymore."

Tâpwê sang Mr. Kaiswatum the song that he'd heard in his dream. He remembered it perfectly.

Mr. Kaiswatum nodded his head as he listened.

"Ho, Tâpwê!" he said when the song was done. "This is a wonderful thing. Nature has taught you some very precious lessons today, and you've learned well. It's like that for all of us, sometimes. We have to make a mistake in order to learn what's right. But you're very young to learn such strong lessons all at once! Do you feel all right now?"

"I feel sad, but at least I don't feel sick in my heart," said Tâpwê. "And you know what?" Tâpwê sounded puzzled. "I'm not mad at Wâpos anymore!"

"That's good, Tâpwê," the old man said. "We already have one Wâpos, and that's enough! Wâpos is just as he should be—the Trickster, and that's all. We also have our one and only Tâpwê, who is just as he should be, I am very glad to say. If Wâpos and Tâpwê were both the same, we should all be poorer for it."

Tâpwê smiled a tearful little smile and hugged Mr.

Kaiswatum shyly. Then he felt something move, up on his head.

"*Chirp?*" he heard.

Tâpwê's smile got bigger. He took off his hat and looked at the little animals in wonder.

"*Chirp! Buzzz! Tweet, whistle! Ch-ch-ch!*" The animals wiggled and fluttered as Tâpwê hugged them.

Tâpwê felt so happy and so grateful that they were all right that he just couldn't say a word. But he didn't have to say anything. His animal friends understood how he was feeling. Remember the Sîwinikan Bear who could send out colors? Tâpwê was sending out love.

Just then, little Brownie the dog trotted up and sat down next to Tâpwê.

"You don't have to do any tricks either, Brownie," Tâpwê said, scratching the dog behind his ears. "We'll always love you because you're such a good friend!"

Mr. Kaiswatum smiled at the boy and the dog.

"Thank you for all the kindling wood, Tâpwê," he said.

"Thank you for helping with my lesson," said Tâpwê. "I think maybe I owe you a few days' work still."

"I'll be very glad to have you around, boy," the old man said. "You come and visit me whenever you want to."

CHAPTER 14

One on Wâpos

ONE MORNING after their chores were all done, Willie and Tâpwê were playing tug-of-war with Brownie, when who should come walking up but Mr. Sam Rockthunder. He was smiling.

"Hello, boys!" he said.

"Hi," said Tâpwê and Willie.

"Willie, I thought you'd like to know, our mama dog came home this morning after hiding on us for quite a while. I thought you might like to see the reason she was hiding."

Willie jumped up. "You mean she has her puppies?"

"You bet!" said Mr. Rockthunder. "Seven pups! We thought she wouldn't have them for another week, but she surprised us. Come and see! You too, Tâpwê."

Willie and Tâpwê followed Mr. Rockthunder over to a place behind his barn. And there they were: seven little puppies, all having breakfast courtesy of their mother, who was lying down on a bed of straw, looking happy. The puppies' eyes were open, but kind of hazy-looking.

"Are they blind?" asked Tâpwê.

"No," said Mr. Rockthunder, "the pups are just young. They haven't had their eyes open that long. In a while their eyes will look normal. They'll be more playful too."

"Oh, look," said Tâpwê. "They're going to sleep."

"Can I hold one?" Willie asked.

"Well, they're a little too young yet. Better wait," Mr. Rockthunder said. "Let's say the day after tomorrow you can come and pick one out. But they'll still have to stay with their mother for a few more weeks. We'll let them sleep now."

On their way back home, Willie and Tâpwê made up a lot of dog names. Then they had a race to the front steps of Willie's house. Then Tâpwê said, "I know! Let's make some arrows and a bow and practice shooting."

So that's what they did.

Now, instead of making their arrows sharp like real ones, Willie and Tâpwê found some sticky pine pitch and stuck it on each arrow tip. They wanted their arrows to stick *to* the targets instead of sticking *into* them.

Then off they went, down toward the stream in the coulee with the little snakes from the Magic Hat riding in Tâpwê's pocket, just like old times. Brownie, the Dog-with-Three-Names, kept them company. Sometimes he pretended he was a wolf, but then he'd forget and go back to being a dog again.

They were walking along beside the stream when Tâpwê poked Willie.

"Look!" he whispered. "There's your sisters."

Tâpwê and Willie ducked into the trees and peeked out. Some girls were down by the stream, with their backs turned to the boys. They were babysitting four little babies wrapped up in blankets. The babies were all sleeping on the grass while the girls washed clothes.

Then the two boys saw the Trickster.

"Uh-ohh," Willie said. "Here comes trouble."

Wâpos was sneaking out from the trees up ahead, creeping along as sly as can be. He snuck up behind the girls, who didn't see him, and laid a towel down on the ground beside the babies. Then he bent over and—very gently—picked up one of the babies and laid her down on the towel. Then he picked up a second baby, a boy, and wrapped *him* up in the girl baby's blanket. Then he swapped the next two babies and their clothes and toys and things.

"Let's get out of here!" whispered Willie. "I don't wanna get blamed for this!"

Down in the coulee, the boys found a good tree to use for target practice, just around the bend from where Wâpos and Tâpwê used to play Possum and Bat.

"Let's have a shoot-it-up-in-the-air contest!" said Tâpwê.

"Okay, you go first," said Willie.

Tâpwê's arrow went *way* up in the air and then came down—*plip!*—in a big clump of skunk cabbage.

"Ho-ohh!" Willie teased. "Tâpwê is hungry for salad!"

Through the trees they saw Willie's sisters and their friends, walking down the path to take the babies home. And there, over through the bushes, was Wâpos. He was scuttling along, a safe distance behind the unsuspecting girls.

Willie took the bow and shot his arrow next. Up and up it went, even higher than Tâpwê's had gone. Then Willie's arrow came down—*splop!*—right in a puddle by his foot.

"*Eee-yew!*" Willie laughed. "*Ishhh!*" He was all polka-dotted with mud and making yucky faces.

"Ho!" cried Tâpwê, laughing along with his friend. "We're gonna have to change Willie's name! How about Wee-na-nesh—for 'dirty guy'!"

Now it was Tâpwê's turn again. He lined up his arrow, pulled back the bowstring, and. . .

Just as he let go, he and Willie heard a loud voice, angry as a bear.

"ROSE IRONCHILD, THIS IS NOT MY BABY!" the woman shouted.

Twang! Tâpwê's arrow was in the air. Up and up, and then it started down. . . and down. . . and down. . .

Now all of the other mothers were yelling too.

"THELMA, YOU COME BACK HERE!"

"MISSY!"

"MARLYN!"

And then, from way up in a tree, came the voice of Wâpos.

"*Ee-yow! Yow-ee! Yowee-ouch!*"

And that Wâpos came tumbling down out of his mischief-watching tree, with Tâpwê's sticky-pitch arrow stuck right to the end of his big pink nose!

Willie and Tâpwê laughed and laughed and laughed. They laughed until their sides ached, and then they rolled on the ground and laughed some more, collapsing on each other's shoulders in giggles and hoots when they thought they just couldn't laugh any longer.

Every time Willie or Tâpwê looked over at Wâpos there he'd be, pulling long strings of pine pitch off his nose like bubblegum, and they'd start in laughing again.

Wâpos never mentioned the baby-swapping incident to anyone, or the sticky arrows. He just acted as if none of it had ever happened.

But for days after, every blowing leaf and fluffy dandelion seed, every bug and bit of sand, camped for a time on the gummiest spot in the valley—the end of the Trickster's nose.

CHAPTER 15

Arrows to the Moon

NOT LONG AFTER THE BABY-SWAPPING INCIDENT, Willie Ironchild's relatives went back to their own reserve, taking their tipi with them. The two boys sure were sorry to have to sleep in the house again. It had been so nice sleeping in a tipi. They would untie their bedrolls and get in them. Then they'd giggle and make jokes, and watch the fire die down, and listen to the big kids talk, until finally they'd fall asleep. If they awoke during the night, they could listen for owls or even gaze up at the sky through the smoke hole at the top of the tipi, watching for falling stars. It was beautiful.

One night it had rained a little. Willie's brother Winston adjusted the smoke-hole flap, closing it to the rain, and they'd all listened to the raindrops pitter-patter on the tipi walls. There was a dew cloth to catch the water away so they all stayed nice and dry.

As the last days of summer floated by, those little puppies that Sam Rockthunder's mama dog had brought into the world grew and grew. They could see and hear and they loved to play, and Willie and his brothers and sisters and Tâpwê all had fun petting them and cuddling them and thinking up names. But they were still too little to go on any real adventures.

A few days later Mr. Kaiswatum told Tâpwê and Willie that if they helped him with the stakes and poles, he would put up his old extra tipi, and then Willie and Tâpwê could camp beside his house for a while. The bluebirds and grass snakes and the Dog-with-Three-Names were welcome too.

This made the boys feel very grown-up and happy, even though Mr. Kaiswatum sure was grouchy while they were trying to get the tipi put up right. It fell down twice, but then they finally got it, with the birds and grass snakes singing old songs and twining the tent ropes to the stakes in the ground.

After the tent was up securely, Mr. Kaiswatum told Tâpwê and Willie to wait outside while he went into the house for something. He came back looking happy again, bringing with him a red cloth bundle, a nice braid of sweetgrass, and a smoldering stick from the fire in the house. He went into the tent.

"You can come in now, boys," Mr. Kaiswatum said.

"Before you live in a new place, you should always thank the Creator for all the good things in life, and remember all your relatives in nature. The animals, the trees, the people who came before you, even the babies not born yet—everything!

"Tâpwê, you put on your hat now," Mr. Kaiswatum said.

When Tâpwê had it firmly on his head, Mr. Kaiswatum unwrapped the red cloth bundle, revealing a big, very beautiful feather, which he handed to Tâpwê. "You hold this Eagle Feather. Careful now—it's very special. And you, Willie, you hold this sweetgrass."

Tâpwê felt honored to be asked to help, and he could tell Willie did too.

"Now," Mr. Kaiswatum continued, "I'll burn just a little of the end of the sweetgrass here, so that it smokes nice. And Tâpwê, you fan that sweetgrass smoke over each one of us while I pray."

Mr. Kaiswatum prayed for a long time, nice and loud, while the sweetgrass perfumed the little tent with blessings. Then he pinched out the warm part of the sweetgrass and wrapped up the Eagle Feather again in his medicine bundle.

"Boy, that smells good," said Willie.

"But it makes me kind of lonesome for my mom and kohkom," Tâpwê said. "They burn sweetgrass when we pray too."

"Tâpwê is homesick, eh?" asked Mr. Kaiswatum.

Tâpwê smiled. "Not really," he said, watching Mr. Kaiswatum set up the willow backrest the old man liked to use when he sat on the ground. "Well. . . maybe a little bit now and then," he added.

"Well, that's good," said Mr. Kaiswatum. "I always miss my family too when I haven't seen them for a while."

"I never missed anybody," said Willie, "except maybe my cousins when they go home every time. I never been anyplace."

"Maybe you can go across and visit Tâpwê sometime," said Mr. Kaiswatum.

"tâp-wê!" Willie and Tâpwê said at the same time. "Then we could really have some fun. We could—"

Mr. Kaiswatum interrupted. "But you gotta expect to miss each other a little when you're parted, because you two are good friends," the old man said. "It's natural. And your family would miss you too, Willie, while you were away."

"*Ayyyy*," laughed the boys, kind of embarrassed at their tender feelings.

"Missing someone's not so bad, though," said Mr. Kaiswatum. "Whenever I miss somebody, it gets me to thinking about all the fun we'll have when I see them again, and I like that. It's good to miss your loved ones. Say there, do you boys know the story about the Arrow Chain, and those two young kids who went to the Moon?"

Willie's eyes popped open wide. "No!" he said.

"Tell us," begged Tâpwê, wiggling around and settling into a good spot for listening to a story. The bluebirds and grass snakes gathered in close. Brownie curled up in Willie's lap.

"kayâs," Mr. Kaiswatum began, "it all happened a long time ago. There were these two young fellows. They were about your size, I guess, maybe a little older.

"One summer night the Moon was not quite full, but it was big and very bright, so's you could see real good, even though it was nighttime. These two kids were still outside, playing with their bows and arrows. Their names were Pêyak and Nisto.

"'What a beautiful Moon,' said Pêyak. But that Nisto, he began to laugh at the Moon.

"'That stupid old Moon isn't even full,' he said. 'It looks all lopsided. That dumb Moon looks like the old hat my auntie wears when she goes picking berries! Ha-ha-ha!'"

Tâpwê and Willie giggled too, but they grew quiet when Mr. Kaiswatum began to speak again.

"All of a sudden there came around those boys a real spooky sparkly light. It just shimmered around them, dancing up and down and making a scary noise like *tssss. . . tssssss*. Well, those boys were sure scared now!

"And then Nisto, that rude boy, he just. . . disappeared."

Mr. Kaiswatum stopped talking and looked right at Tâpwê. And then right at Willie. Then he continued.

"Well, now, Pêyak just didn't know what to do. He was more scared than he'd ever been in all his life. He couldn't move, or yell, or anything. All he could think to do was pray in his heart that his friend would come back.

"Then he heard this real strange music, like he'd never heard before, and a voice like hissing steam said, 'Shoot an arrow into the air and aim it at the Moon.'

"'But I love the Moon,' Pêyak said in his heart.

"'I *am* the Moon,' said the voice. 'My name is Tipiskâwi-pîsim. Shoot to me and I will help you.'

"Poor Pêyak was scared. He could hardly aim his arrow, he was shaking so hard, but he did as he was told. His arrow went *way* up and up and up, all the way to the Moon.

"'Shoot another,' said the Moon. So Pêyak shot another arrow, and it too went sailing off, and then. . . *ting!* That arrow stuck right to the end of the first arrow!

"'Shoot a whole chain of arrows, and then you can climb up and rescue your friend-who-has-no-manners, if you like him so much,' said the Moon."

Tâpwê tried to imagine shooting arrows as high as the Moon. When he and Willie shot theirs, they'd only gone as high as the treetops.

"Soon enough," Mr. Kaiswatum continued, "Pêyak found himself climbing through the sky. This world below looked like a little blue turtle shell, it was so far off. At last he reached the Moon.

"'Nisto!' Pêyak hollered. 'tânitê kâ-ayâyan, Nisto? Where are you?'

"Just then Pêyak saw something over in the distance. It was Nisto, running toward Pêyak as fast as he could run! And chasing him was a big, spinning whirlwind, the kind that some people call a dust devil.

"Pêyak ducked down into a crack in some rocks, and

when Nisto got to him he grabbed his friend by the legs and pulled him into safety. The whirlwind passed by.

"Nisto was very glad that the Moon had helped Pêyak to come and rescue him. He had never known that the Moon was so powerful. To Nisto the Moon had only been a light in the nighttime sky. But now he knew that the Moon was alive and had feelings, just like all the other creatures of the Creator.

"'I want you to apologize to the Moon for me,' Nisto told Pêyak.

"'You'd better do that yourself, or you'll miss the healing,' Pêyak said, giving his friend some sweetgrass from his pouch.

"Nisto peeked out from their hiding place in the rocks. All was quiet, so he climbed out. He burned a little sweetgrass and sang the only prayer song he knew, the one his father always sang when he prayed. He sang it four times through, facing in each of the four directions. And as he prayed, he was thinking in his heart how silly he'd been to tell a lie about the Moon. Everybody knows the Moon is beautiful.

"Well, boys, Pêyak and Nisto were sure glad to get home again. They'd been gone for a long time. When

they came walking into camp, one little girl thought they were ghosts and went hollering to her mother. But soon everybody had heard about their adventure and knew that it was really Pêyak and Nisto, safely returned. Their families were so happy they gave a feast to give thanks to all the people who'd prayed for the boys. Of course, everybody was invited, and the families gave away lots of nice presents. That's how it was in the old days around here. It was a real honor to give things away when you were thankful for your life."

Mr. Kaiswatum stretched. "That's all of that story for now, boys," he said.

"You mean there's more?" asked Willie.

"Oh my, yes," said Mr. Kaiswatum. "Pêyak and Nisto had all kinds of adventures up there on the Moon. But those stories are for some other time. I'm going in for a nap now."

"Thanks for the story," Willie said. He and Brownie the Dog-with-Three-Names both stretched.

Willie and Tâpwê and Brownie and the baby grass snakes and the bluebirds all fell asleep in the tipi. Everybody had real good dreams that afternoon.

CHAPTER 16

Four Sacred Colors

WELL, THE WEATHER WAS BEGINNING to turn cool, changing the forests into colors like a thousand Sîwinikan Bears, and soon the afternoon arrived when Kohkom came to bring Tâpwê home. Tâpwê had spent two whole mornings gathering wood as his goodbye presents to his new friends here and there around the reserve. Now it was afternoon and he felt ready for a nap. But then Kohkom arrived and they had a little something to eat with everybody—everybody but Willie, that is. He wasn't there.

Soon it was time for Tâpwê to begin saying his goodbyes.

He gave each of his friends a feather from his hat, and also a word of advice. "Watch out for Tricksters!" he told them, and they all laughed. Everybody knew that old Wâpos had given Tâpwê some experiences he'd never forget.

Mrs. Loudhawk gave Tâpwê a fresh braid of sweetgrass, and Mrs. Cheechuck gave him some of her famous chokecherries.

Mr. Kaiswatum invited Tâpwê into his house and gave

him an Eagle Feather that he'd found in a secret place. He'd been saving it to give to someone special, he said, and he thought Tâpwê was just the one.

"You come back and visit us again, Tâpwê. The people will teach you a lot of good things, and learn from you too," Mr. Kaiswatum said. "That's how we are around here. Do you still remember that song you heard the Eagles sing to you about dancing to your own heartbeat?"

"Uh-huh," said Tâpwê seriously. "I will never forget that."

"Good!" Mr. Kaiswatum said. "That's good, boy. That's your song. When you come back, we'll have a name-giving ceremony for you. You think about that until we see you again.

"You know," Mr. Kaiswatum continued, "when I was a young man, I received a sacred song too. I'm gonna pray for you now and sing you my song."

Mr. Kaiswatum burned a little sweetgrass like he always did before he prayed. Then he took out his small drum and his drumstick and put them in his lap.

"kihci-manitow," he began, and then he prayed in his own language, just talking to the Creator like a loving child talks to his parent, so easy and nice. And then he began to sing in the real old style:

misiwêskamik
nitâpwêyihtên
Way ya   way way ya
Way ya   way way ya
Way ya   way way ya

When Mr. Kaiswatum was done singing, Tâpwê asked
him about Wâpos one more time.

"I was just wondering," he said, "about how poor Wâpos
is always so worried about being the most important."

"Nobody is the most important around here, Tâpwê,"
Mr. Kaiswatum said. "But as for Wâpos, that Trickster. . .
he's already very important. He is the one who keeps us on
our toes for mischief—especially in ourselves! You know!"

Tâpwê sure did know.

When Tâpwê got back to the Ironchild house, Thelma
had wrapped up some frybreads for him and his kohkom
to take along.

"*Ayyyy!*" Tâpwê said. "I sure hope I don't open this
package and find horsebuns instead."

"Tâpwê, you better keep checking the side of your

head." Thelma laughed. "All the time you spent with Wâpos, I wouldn't be surprised if you show up next year with long fuzzy ears!"

"Or walking upside down from too much Possum and Bat!" teased Winston.

Auntie Lilian was looking out the windows now, one by one.

"Oh, where's that Willie?" she said. "I know he doesn't want to miss telling you goodbye, Tâpwê!"

"Come on, Tâpwê," said Kohkom. "We have a long road ahead. We'd better get going."

Tâpwê put on his Magic Hat and strapped his quiver of sticky-pitch arrows and his bow onto his back. He treasured them, because he knew that whenever he looked at the bow and arrows, he would remember his friends from the reserve, including Wâpos.

The Ironchild children all walked along with Tâpwê and Kohkom, down the path that led to the trail out of the valley and to the road beyond. When they came around the bend in the path, there stood Willie, holding in his arms the new puppy that Sam Rockthunder had given him.

"I want to name my puppy Tâpwê, if it's okay with you, Tâpwê," Willie said.

Tâpwê smiled his big smile. "Sure, it's okay," he said. He put his cheek next to the puppy, who sniffed and kissed Tâpwê and then sneezed, the way that puppies do. Tâpwê laughed. The animals on the Magic Hat danced happily.

Just then Sam and his mama dog came up to them. Sam held another puppy in his arms, the spotted one that Tâpwê liked the best. Willie put his own puppy down next to the mama dog, then reached over to Sam and lifted that little spotted dog into Tâpwê's arms.

"Here you go, Tâpwê, this one's all yours," Willie said.

"Chaa," whispered Tâpwê, cuddling that puppy who nuzzled his cheek with his cool little nose as if each of them thought the other were the greatest treasure on earth. "Really, is he for me? Can I bring him home?" he asked, looking at Kohkom.

Kohkom was all smiles. "Sure," she said, reaching over to give the little puppy a scratch behind his ear. "We'll make it work."

Tâpwê looked around the circle of good friends, people and animals, and felt so grateful in his heart. "kihci-mîkwêc," he said, "to all of you." He smiled his real smile and all the animals on the Magic Hat tweeted and rattled and sang.

Tâpwê felt something pulling at the quiver of bows and arrows that were strapped over his shoulder. The bluebirds were unfastening it and whispering an idea to Tâpwê.

He reached over his shoulder and took off the bow and quiver of arrows. The bluebirds lifted them up and flew them right over to Willie as a gift.

"I'll never forget you, Willie," Tâpwê said, shaking Willie's hand one time like the old people do.

"Me too," said Willie. "Come on back same time next year for the powwow. I'm gonna dance!"

Everybody had one last hug. And then Tâpwê and Kohkom were off on their journey.

As they walked to the truck, they heard a familiar voice, way off in the distance on the other side of the reserve. It was singing, "*TRICK-ster Ha-Yaa-Yaaa!*" Tâpwê knew that Wâpos was up to his usual pranks, and he wondered who had learned a lesson this time.

Back in the truck, Tâpwê and that little pup snuggled up fast, all full of good ideas. Kohkom started to ask Tâpwê to tell some more about his adventures, but Tâpwê was yawning a big yawn. The little grass snakes were curled up beneath the bluebirds' folded wings, and

Tâpwê's puppy was snoring sweet little puppy snores in a nest of love and feathers.

Tâpwê looked over at Kohkom, and she smiled and said, "I'm so glad to have you and these little friends back with me again."

She looked ahead at the late afternoon golden sky and at the braid of sweetgrass that Tâpwê had placed on the dashboard in front of her.

"I guess I'll have to wait until tomorrow to hear about your adventures," she said to the sleepy boy.

As Tâpwê drifted off, he heard her start to pray.

"kihci-manitow, Great Spirit: thank you for the yellow of the turning trees. . . the white of the sage in the fields. . . the black of Tâpwê's hair. . . and the red of the sunset. Four sacred colors.

"Thank you," she said again. "kihci-mîkwêc, kihci-manitow!"

Note to Parents and Teachers

Tâpwê and the Magic Hat is a work of contemporary fiction.

It should not be presented to children as an "authentic" legend in the historical sense of that word, although the people in the story are all based on real people I know well, and they are all reserve-born Indigenous North American people.

Some of the stories that old Mr. Kaiswatum tells are traditional stories, however, and they are still told today as they have been told for generations. These stories vary a bit from one Indigenous nation to another.

Since Indigenous people travel around a lot learning about one another's cultures, so do our stories, songs, sayings, dress styles, et cetera travel across cultural and even international "borders." The real Mr. Kaiswatum was a Plains Cree man from Saskatchewan, Canada, but he also wore a Navajo ring from Arizona when he felt like it.

Trickster stories are found in many Indigenous North American nations. Sometimes the traditional Trickster takes the form of Coyote, or Raven, or is known simply as the Trickster, or by an individual name in the languages of the people (wîsahkêcâhk to many of the Cree language groups, Inktumni to the Assiniboines, et cetera).

In *Tâpwê and the Magic Hat*, our Wâpos character is a greatly toned down version of the Trickster. The traditional Trickster is most often much more than just a mischief-maker. He can be both childlike and adult in character, and can border on the malevolent and even erotic. But just as often, the Trickster is simply naughty, foolish, mischievous, and silly, as he is here.

Since *Tâpwê and the Magic Hat* is a story for children, I've portrayed the Trickster in his more childish moments, as Wâpos the Rabbit.

Libraries, particularly those at universities that offer a Native Studies program, have lots of books about the real traditional Trickster, if you'd like to know more.

I wrote this book over a number of years as my son was growing up. Many thanks to the Piapot-Obey families for your love and for all of the adventures we have had together.

—Buffy Sainte-Marie

Glossary

Note: In Cree language materials spelled using the alphabet (in what is called the standard roman orthography), there are no capital letters. For ease of reading in this English-language version of the story, capital letters are used for Cree character names.

CREE (NÊHIYAW) WORD	TRANSLATION	PRONUNCIATION
âhâsiw	crow	AH-hah-siw
An chaa! (from ânakacâ)	yikes; my goodness!	ahn-chah (AH nuk kuh CHAH)
âstam	come	aas-TUM
Kaiswatum (Mr.)	character's surname	kaysh-ay-wah-tum
kâsakês	greedy guts	KAH-suh-kays

kayâs	once upon a time	ka-YAAS
kihci	very much, very great	keeh tsih
kihci-manitow	Great Spirit (God)	keeh-tsih-MUN-(i)-toh
kohkom	grandmother	KOH-koom
*megwetch (mîkwêc)	thank you	me-GWETCH / me GWAYTCH
mîcisotân	eat	mee-CHIS-so-taan / MEETS-so-taan
misiwêskamik	everywhere, all over the world	miss-ih-WAYS-kuh-mick
nêhiyaw	Cree, Cree person	NAY hee yow
nisto	three	nis-TOO
nitâpwêhtên	I believe, I believe it	nih-TAA-pwayh-tayn

okimâw	leader, chief	OH-kim-maw
pêyak	one	pay-YUK
piyêsîs	bird	PEE-yay-sees
sîwinikan	sweet sugar	see-WIN-nig-gan
tânisi	hello	TAN-(i)-si
tânitê kâ-ayâyan?	where are you?	TAH-n(ih)-tay KAA-yaa-yun?
tâpwê	yes, indeed; you bet	tah-PWAY
tipiskâwi-pîsim	moon	tip-pihs-KAH-wih-pee-sim
wâpos	rabbit	wa-POOS
Way heyo hey yo	singing sounds like *la-la*	WAY hay-yoh hay-YOH

**Wee-na-nesh   dirty guy   wee-na-NESH

---

*megwetch is a borrow word from the Anishinabe which the Cree have freely adopted. One of the Cree words, the one used in common situations, is "kinanâskomitin—I thank you."

**This may also be a Saulteaux form of the word, whereas a Plains Cree version of the word might more likely have the form wînis [wee NISS]

Other words to know:

Coulee: a small ravine or gully

Horsebuns: horse poop

Sweetgrass: a fragrant long grass that grows in marshy places and is braided, burned as a prayer incense, and carried by travelers when away from home

Buffy Sainte-Marie has made her voice heard
through her music, art, and activism, establishing herself
among the ranks of great songwriters. Her long career
has seen her rise to stardom on the folk circuit with
forays into country, rock, soundtracks, acting, activism,
and children's television. Now, she adds children's book
author to her incredible list of accomplishments.

Michelle Alynn Clement is an award-winning book
designer and illustrator from Vancouver, BC. She works
from a quiet, colorful little studio that's filled to the
brim with books, and loves drawing, imagining, colors,
collecting, getting lost in nature, hammocks, and reading.
She's still just as intrigued by the magic of folk stories,
fairy tales, and fables, and all sorts of other wondrous,
unexplainable happenings, as she was growing up.